DIANA
The Children's Princess

DIANA
The Children's Princess

Harriet Storey

Michael Joseph
London

First published in Great Britain in 1984 by Michael Joseph Ltd
44 Bedford Square, London WC1

British Library Cataloguing in Publication Data

Storey, Harriet
Diana, the children's princess.
1. Diana, *Princess of Wales* 2. Great Britain—Princes and princesses—Biography
I. Title
941.085′092′4 DA591.A45D5

ISBN 0-7181-2503-7

Designed and produced by
The Rainbird Publishing Group Ltd,
40 Park Street, London W1Y 4DE

House Editor: Rachel Stewart
Designer: Martin Bristow

Text filmset by Bookworm Typesetting, Manchester, England
Colour origination by Gilchrist Brothers Ltd, Leeds, England
Printed and bound by Ambassador Press Ltd, St. Albans, England

Half-title: *The Princess of Wales and Prince William at home in Kensington Palace.*
Frontispiece: *Shy admirers meet the Princess of Wales in Wellington, New Zealand.*

Illustration Acknowledgments

The publishers would like to thank the following who have supplied pictures for reproduction in this book:

Mrs R.V.M. Anderson, New Malden: 90; Camera Press Ltd – Photo Patrick Lichfield: 11; Keystone Press Agency Ltd: 23, 29, 57 (right), 58, 60, 61, 62, 65; Tim Graham: 1, 2, 7, 12, 13 (both), 14, 15 (both), 17, 19 (both), 20 (both), 21, 24-5, 26 (both), 28, 30-1, 32, 33, 34 (right), 35, 36 (both), 37, 38, 40, 41, 50, 54 (left), 59 (both), 63 (both), 69 (both), 70, 71, 72, 73, 74-5, 76, 77 (both), 78, 80, 81, 82, 85, 87, 88 (both), 89, 91 (top), 92, 93 (below), 95, 96 (both); Anwar Hussein: 42, 43, 53, 57 (left), 67, 79; Rosie Oxley's Collection: 44-49; Photographers International: 34 (left), 39; Rainbird Picture Library: 93; Rex Features: 27, 54 (right), 55; Russell Whitehurst, Yass, Australia: 91.

Contents

CHAPTER ONE

A Radiant Mother

Those who imagined that the fuss over the Princess of Wales' offspring had reached its peak of hype and hysteria at the birth of her first child, Prince William, were disappointed on the 13 February 1984 when the Palace announced her second pregnancy. 'Secret Behind That Smile – A Baby!' enthused the *Daily Mail*. 'Smile That Says It All,' said the *Daily Express*. 'Happy Di Wants A Girl,' said the *Sun*, and the *Star* headlined the news 'September Baby For Diana And Charles – So Much In Love'.

To the unquenchable amazement of anti-monarchists, congratulatory crowds turned up outside Kensington Palace, the bookmakers' wires started buzzing and Sir Ronald Gardner-Thorpe who, as Lord Mayor of London at the time of the announcement of the Princess' first pregnancy, had come up with 'Babies are bits of stardust blown from the hand of God', rose to the occasion again with 'A lovely being scarcely formed or moulded; A rose with all its sweetest leaves unfolded.'

The timing of the announcement was perfect. As one royal observer said: 'Prince Charles and the Princess are so much in love they wanted to share their wonderful news for Valentine's Day with all the world's romantics.' But amongst the babble of baby talk, there was one voice of dissent. Professor Harold Francis, a senior gynaecologist at the Liverpool Women's Hospital, felt that if the Princess of Wales intended to have many more children, it could have catastrophic consequences. The 'baby boom' of the 60s, he gravely explained, was to be attributed partly to mothers following The Queen's example of four. The prospect of a 'Diana baby boom' he found horrifying. 'A third child would mean a crisis for the country, the obstetric service, the schools, and more importantly, the job situation,' he said. He even took it upon himself to suggest that the Prince and Princess should consider sterilization.

The last man who had hit the news with similar views on the evils of population growth was, ironically enough, Prince Philip, father of those very four, who on a visit to the Solomon Islands chose to air his views on their rapidly rising birth rate in the cheerful setting of a local maternity unit. 'Five per cent – five per cent – you must be out of your minds,' he said. 'You'll have a massive economic crisis in 20 years time and blame everybody else.'

According to the Palace, he did not share Professor Francis' doubts about the new royal infant. Nor did anyone else. At bus stops all over the country on the morning of 13 February the talk was not of the newly appointed Soviet leader, but of Diana's pregnancy. Politics were forgotten in the face of an important family event. For a royal marriage, death or birth are as important to the people of Britain as a marriage, death or birth in their own family.

In Russia, *Pravda* found the fuss made over Prince William sickening. 'If you sat close enough to the television you did not need sugar in your tea,' it reported, after the six-month-old Prince had been presented to

Right: Relaxed, and brimming with pleasure in each other's company, Diana and Prince William of Wales bring a new informal image to royal motherhood for the 1980s. The smiles were on the eve of the royal visit to Australia and New Zealand, when the Prince was only nine months old.

Above: First glimpses of the then Lady Diana Spencer firmly imprinted in the public's mind the fact that she adored small children. Here she is with two of the children she helped care for at the Young England Kindergarten School in Pimlico. The date was September 1980, when the school was suddenly besieged by the press.

the cameras at Christmas 1982, adding that it would be better if the papers concentrated on the poor masses, which did not, like him, have a little silver boomerang to play with. In Britain, however, there is every evidence that 'the masses', poor and rich, are united in their delight at the sight of Prince William and his family, with or without silver boomerangs.

As *The Times* meditated in its leader at Christmas 1983: 'One of the functions of the monarchy in our national life is to represent the significance of family life. The circulation of nursery photographs and sentimental information about how the youngsters are coming on is as much a part of that function nationally as it is to the lives of any other family.' Anyone who doubts the strength of affection between the public and the monarchy need only watch the reactions of the crowds when a member of the Royal Family goes walkabout. Near hysterical enthusiasm at the approach of one of the Royals often gives way to tears of happiness on the part of those who have been spoken to – especially if the Royal concerned is The Queen or her daughter-in-law.

At the slightest hint of a problem in the royal household the nation weighs in with understanding and affection – in fact mothers identify so

Above: Proof that Prince William takes after his mother in looks, as well as his grandfather Earl Spencer, who took this picture of his strong-minded youngest daughter in her pram. 'As a baby she could have won any beauty competition,' her father said of Diana. Like William she had a nanny to take care of her.

strongly with Diana that they write reassuringly to the papers, and to her, telling her not to worry about the things that once perplexed them. The intense interest in the Wales' domestic life suggest that Victorian family values are cherished as much today as they were in the nineteenth century.

If the representation of enduring family life is now one of the chief functions of constitutional monarchy, perhaps one of the reasons why the Princess of Wales, of all the members of the Royal Family, produces such an astonishing response, is that she manages to convey an image that combines the height of glamour with the most touching domesticity. Beautiful, rich and aristocratic by birth, she nevertheless makes it perfectly plain that for her, the ordinary job of being a wife and mother is what really counts.

The association in the mind of the public between Diana and children was made at the very moment the lady was first introduced to them as a likely future Queen of England, in that now legendary shot of her with the sun shining through her cotton skirt and a toddler on her hip. It splendidly summed up the combination of allure and maternal care that Diana has been projecting ever since. Before that moment no Fleet Street editor could ever have believed that such an image could hold more appeal and become more successful at selling papers than any page three siren.

Diana's arrival in the news came at the end of two decades when women had claimed headlines for their brazen sex appeal or for their success in their careers. Diana did not fit into either category. Her sex appeal is demure, alluring and unselfconscious – the very opposite of brazen. And her career achievements as a single girl were unspectacular. She was brought up in a highly conservative fashion in the old traditions of the British upper classes, with the emphasis in her education put on good manners, responsibility and the hope of a good husband, rather than good examination results. But she had no modern qualms about her role in life. From the moment of her engagement, when she appeared on television saying that with Charles to tell her what to do, she was sure she'd be all right, she revived the image of the nice, old-fashioned girl who had so long been out of the news. Her adoration for children was immediately obvious. She had worked as an assistant in the Young England kindergarten in Pimlico, and spent over a year looking after Patrick, the two-year-old son of an American couple. The public was instantly convinced that she was every mother's ideal daughter and every child's ideal mother.

From the way she picked up, cuddled and kissed the children she met on her post-engagement walkabouts, it was clear that her addiction to them was perfectly sincere. And she made no secret of the fact that she wanted lots of children of her own. Right from the very start, Diana really was the Children's Princess.

Her affinity with children was obviously one of the reasons Prince Charles chose her as his bride. He had already had a long list of girlfriends whose names read like a roll-call from Debrett's Peerage. Though all were suitable companions for an heir to the throne, only three really stood out as contenders for future Queen. These were

Davina Sheffield, Lady Sarah Spencer and the bookies' favourite, Lady Jane Wellesley.

As Charles' romances with these three cooled to friendship, attention turned to glamorous Princess Caroline and Catholic Princess Marie-Astrid, whose blue blood put them firmly in the running. But Charles ruled them out as incompatible. He knew just what he wanted: 'Marriage is a much more important business than falling in love... it's all about creating a secure family unit in which to bring up children. You have to remember that when you marry in my position, you're going to marry someone who is perhaps one day going to be Queen. You've got to choose someone very carefully, who could fill this particular role, and it has got to be someone pretty unusual.'

Charles also had to choose with exceptional care, because his is a marriage in which divorce is unthinkable, and as such an even more powerful symbol of family life than most. At the Royal Wedding on 29 July 1981 there was no room for cynical predictions, and the ceremony was lent even more poignancy by the sight of the Princess of Wales' divorced parents briefly united in St Paul's for their daughter's wedding. The wedding also reinforced, by its many child attendants, the link between the Princess of Wales and children. Apart from the famous kiss, one of the most charming moments on the balcony was the sight of Diana hand in hand with the youngest bridesmaid, Clementine Hambro, five years old, who had been one of her charges at the Young England kindergarten.

There was no doubt, right from the very first, that married life suited Diana down to the ground. Her honeymoon statement that marriage was wonderful – 'I highly recommend it' – was only to be hoped for from a bride of a few weeks, but even two years later in October 1983, when she met Barry Manilow at a charity concert at the Festival Hall, her talk was all of marriage and how much good it would do him. 'Get married and put some weight on,' she advised him. 'You really should have someone to look after you.' Even Barry was impressed by this concern. 'She was really sweet,' he told reporters later. 'She told me at least five times during our conversation that I ought to be married.'

The same enthusiasm was expressed in November 1982 to Margaret Younger, a resident of the Royal School for the Blind at Leatherhead, Surrey, when Diana called to open an extension. 'Married life is wonderful,' said the Princess, when she heard that Margaret was planning to marry another resident. Afterwards a delighted Miss Younger commented: 'That's the best advice anyone could have.' And Diana dished out more positive advice on a visit to Stoke Mandeville Hospital. 'Are you marrying?' she asked Mick Sorrell, who had been paralysed in a driving accident, when she saw him fondly talking to Wendy Hudson. When the couple seemed indecisive she told them briskly how splendid matrimony was. 'That', said Wendy, as she came out of the church door beneath a firemans' arch early in 1984, 'made up our minds. We had been thinking of getting married but after speaking to her we had no doubts left.'

On the subject of the bliss of marriage the Princess is indefatigable, which must be doing wonders for the ego of the Prince of Wales, if not for his figure. 'She keeps trying to feed me up,' he has been heard to say, confirming that her remarks to Mr Manilow were no jest.

When, a few months after the wedding, she became pregnant, her very evident pleasure, despite some alarm at the loss of her recently acquired slim figure and the unpleasantness of prolonged morning sickness, was in marked contrast to the attitude of her sister-in-law Princess Anne the year before when she was pregnant with Zara. There was a critical reaction to Anne's typically ironic, self-deprecatory remarks in a 40-minute television documentary, which showed her with Captain Phillips in their Gatcombe Park home. 'I'm not particularly maternal in outlook,' she said, playing down her obvious affection for young Peter and her astonishing and tireless commitment to the Save The Children Fund. She thought that the main part of her pregnancy was 'a very boring six months' and added wryly: 'It's an occupational hazard if you're a wife.'

Next day righteous indignation ran loose among the press, placing unwarranted interpretations on Anne's remarks and demanding to know what right a privileged Princess had to sneer at motherhood when there were so many unfortunate women around who would give anything to be in the state she found so boring.

There was no chance of misinterpreting the Princess of Wales' attitude to pregnancy. From the beginning her delight was evident. And, from the beginning, because William had been conceived so soon after

Below: Always surrounded by children, Diana made no exception for her wedding, where she starred in the midst of five bridesmaids and two pageboys. Here five-year-old Clementine Hambro, great-granddaughter of Sir Winston Churchill, and one of the children Diana had looked after in the Pimlico kindergarten, receives a quick word of reassurance before the balcony scene on the wedding day.

Right: In the early months of her first pregnancy Diana was plagued by sickness. In November, on a visit to Chester, she looked pale and very tired, to the evident concern of her husband. 'Some days I feel terrible,' she told a woman in the crowd.

her marriage, while public interest in her was still insatiable, the Princess of Wales became the first member of the Royal Family to have a highly media-visible pregnancy.

Every trace of paleness, every sign of morning sickness was anxiously reported and overnight, gynaecologists became sibyls, to be questioned at every stage for pronouncements about whether the Princess was under too much stress, whether it was wise for her to have a home birth, and – inevitably – what the chances were of her having twins.

So keen was the public's interest in Diana that reporters and photographers, including the legendary James Whitaker, were despatched to crawl through the undergrowth of the Caribbean to catch sight of the pregnant Princess in her bikini. Charles and Diana were staying at the house of Lord Mountbatten's grandson, Lord Romsey, on the island of Windermere. After a dash through the jungle with the film and the story, where by his own account Mr Whitaker showed courage and resilience against near impossible odds which would have done justice to a hardened war reporter, the blurred and highly unflattering shots were wired back to London to appear next day in the *Sun*, while another set, taken from a few yards away, were published in the *Star*. The papers sold out, and an outcry resulted. There was general agreement that this was taking an interest in the royal domestic life and the Princess' pregnancy too far.

More decorous photographs of the pregnant Princess appeared right up to the last few days before she gave birth – unthinkable at the time of The Queen's pregnancies. Her last public engagement, five weeks before the birth, was to open the Albany Community Centre in Deptford. And Diana's appearance in those later months, when she continued to look both glamorous and healthy, was a marvellous proof that expectant mothers today need not feel pregnancy is a shameful and disfiguring state. The Princess more than lived up to the challenge to appear at her best. It was not just her tall figure that helped her to look so good, though a height of 5' 10" was no disadvantage. She managed, when she assembled her wardrobe for the crucial six months, not to fall into the trap of buying the usual apologetic flowery smocks, but instead adapted her own style to her new shape.

Her low pumps were already ideal for pregnancy, and so were the deep white sailor collars and big artists' bows she had made into a trademark from the beginning. Like her chokers, they focussed attention on her face. In a series of clear, fresh-coloured silk day dresses from

Below left: In the last months the Princess of Wales, suntanned and cheerful, was visibly delighting in the imminent prospect of a baby. 'I'm hoping for a boy,' she told a questioner in the crowd on 18 May when she opened the Albany Community Centre – her last public engagement before the birth.
Below right: Relaxed and in the pink for a visit to a game of polo at Smith's Lawn, Windsor, in June. She chose her famous gold 'D' pendant to go with a dress which unblushingly drew attention to her pregnancy.

Left: The children of St Mary's were so pleased to see the Duchess of Cornwall on her April visit to the Scilly Isles in 1982 that they gave her no less than 74 posies.
Above left: Witty and comfortable – Diana gives new inspiration to maternity fashion in her koala jumper at a polo match in May.
Above right: Very simple lines, eye-catching detail at the neck and on the hat, and sensibly low heels for Diana's appearance at Ascot in June.

favourite designers such as Belville Sassoon and Jasper Conran, she looked wonderful, especially as, in the last few months, she was deeply sun-tanned and glowing with happiness.

Crowds thrilled to see her flouting the tradition of 'confinement' and turning up on the first day of Royal Ascot – a mere six days before the birth – in yards of palest peach and a pillbox, looking stunning. She solved the problem of being pregnant in formal evening dress by choosing historically inspired gowns from a period when fuller figures were the rage, like the Stuart style deep red taffeta gown Belville Sassoon made for her, with a high waist, low neckline and lace at neck and cuffs, which she wore, glittering with diamonds, at the Barbican Arts Centre in March. By proving so convincingly that pregnancy need not be a dowdy state, Diana did every woman a service.

But perhaps she looked most engaging of all informally clad for one of Charles' polo engagements, in an enormous, brightly coloured sweater with a koala bear design, which was knitted for her husband by an Australian fan. It was an inspired and an inspiring choice. A popular paper ran a knitting pattern of it and maternity wear buyers began looking around for a good supplier of bright, amusing knitwear. Fun, something long missing from most maternity wear shops, was suddenly fashionable. Instead of concealing it, the koala bear woolly drew attention to the Princess' bump. Once again, Diana started a new trend in fashion, this time appealing additionally to the many women who now choose to have their first child at a later age, and are thrilled by the prospect of pregnancy instead of taking it as a matter of course.

At five a.m. on 21 June 1982 the nation was on tenterhooks as the Princess of Wales was driven with her husband to St Mary's Hospital, Paddington. She was in the early stages of labour and was admitted to a special room in the Lindo Wing. Her baby was the first heir to the throne to be born in hospital.

Outside the building crowds of wellwishers and press gathered, and they stayed the whole day despite a continual drizzle. The Princess' labour lasted 16 hours, and Charles was at her side throughout. He was present at the birth of their son at 9.03 that evening, Midsummer's Day. Diana's gynaecologist, George Pinker, confirmed that it had been a nearly natural birth. 'Yes it was ... well, almost. Just at the end the Princess did have a bit of pain relief, but I'm afraid I can't go into details.' The baby's father was overwhelmed by the event and admitted, on his emergence from the hospital, that being a father was 'rather a grownup thing. Rather a shock to my system.'

At Buckingham Palace the traditional notice announcing the arrival of the second in line to the throne was posted behind the gates. William weighed 7lb 1½oz, cried lustily and had a wisp of fair hair and blue eyes. Inside the Palace his royal grandparents celebrated with champagne, while telegrams bearing the news of the birth were sent to the four corners of the earth. The Archbishop of Canterbury, Dr Robert Runcie, proclaimed: 'We rejoice with them. It is good news for millions around the world who hold them in their affection and their prayers.' And The Queen ordered a personal tribute of two 41-gun salutes to be fired at one o'clock the following day.

Before their short stay in hospital was over, Diana and her son were visited by her parents, Mrs Shand Kydd and Earl Spencer. 'She is looking radiant, absolutely radiant,' said Diana's mother. 'My grandson is a lovely baby. There is a great deal of happiness in there.' The Princess' father enthused: 'He is the most beautiful baby I have ever seen.'

The modern mother began as she meant to go on, leaving hospital only 36 hours after her arrival to a tumultuous reception from the crowds outside. As the couple appeared on the steps of the Lindo Wing, Charles passed the baby to his wife. The gesture was perfect. They were a family.

Only a year later, while the country was reaffirming its enthusiasm for Diana's firstborn by sending over 1000 birthday cards to a Prince at the tearing rather than the reading stage, and Charles was celebrating with a cake that weighed more than the boy himself, royal watchers were already speculating on a new pregnancy for the Princess.

The game had begun the month before William's birthday, when on the authority of no less a person than Prince Charles' ex-valet, Stephen Barry, gossip columnist Nigel Dempster announced that if she were not

Above: Some day my prince will come – Diana and Charles, the day after the baby prince arrived, leaving St Mary's Hospital, Paddington for Kensington Palace.

already pregnant, she would become so by the autumn. Earl Spencer nurtured the rumour by hoping out loud that all three of his daughters would present him with a new grandchild that year. But talk of what was excrutiatingly called 'a nappy event' did not really take off until June, when Prince Charles made an unfortunate public joke about 'the royal breeding programme'. It was, he said, 'firmly underway'.

The Palace switchboard was besieged. Official statements that the remark was merely humorous were not helped a few days later at a Windsor polo match, when Chief Inspector Colin Trimming, asked why Diana was not with Charles, stepped out of his role as personal detective and into that of court jester with his response: 'This morning sickness does terrible things to you.'

It was probably less of a joke to the Princess herself, who found all eyes on her waistline. A few pounds on, a trace of a smile, and flickering interest about her 'pregnancy' became a forest fire. But if she *lost* a few pounds and became super-slim, the word went round that Diana, like her sister Sarah before her, was annorexic and therefore, rumour impertinently concluded, probably unable to have a baby. Diana put her own foot in it days after the polo joke when she visited a hospital in Preston and made headlines once more by innocently asking if there was a German measles epidemic there. 'The disease can harm unborn children if the mother comes into contact with it early in pregnancy,' reported the *Daily Express* significantly.

Speculation died down over the summer, but by autumn, with the excitement of the Canadian tour and William's first birthday over, the public and the papers were ready for another guessing game. It was given the perfect start when the Princess flew back from Balmoral for a day early in September, just as she had done at the start of her first pregnancy two years previously. It happened to be on the same day that her gynaecologist returned to work from his holidays. Speculation ran rife, but the real reason for the Princess' trip was a mundane one – she was en route to her hairdresser, Kevin Shanley.

In the ensuing though unwarranted hubbub, members of the public proved that they too were interested in playing the part of amateur gynaecologist and pregnancy spotter. 'We are very curious to know if you are having a baby,' said a factory girl called Elaine Robertson when she met Diana at the Keiller marmalade and sweet plant in Dundee. And the papers, desperate for any straws in the wind, turned to that old standby, 'women's intuition', for confirmation. They were delighted when Elaine declared firmly that the Princess was pregnant. Valerie Gowans, aged 26, agreed. 'Definitely,' she said, cuddling her seven-month-old daughter Jennifer. The Princess, she pointed out, was not only 'gorgeous' but 'blooming', a sure sign that another little Wales was on the way. Elaine's declaration was pounced upon by James Whittaker, the royal journalist extraordinaire. Using a considerable amount of imagination, he described a party to celebrate the news of her new pregnancy. 'The Royal Family were delighted and called for champagne to celebrate,' he wrote. 'I am told there was a lot of kissing at the same time, followed by a very jolly dinner party.'

Diana's cross press secretary Victor Chapman immediately issued a firm denial. Nevertheless the rumours continued into October. By November there were speculations on the chance of twins in 1984, on the grounds that Diana's aunt on her father's side had had them, her grandmother on her mother's side was one of a pair, and her aunt on the same side had also produced a double. The mere idea of the amount of extra attention the arrival of the first pair of royal twins for centuries would produce is so exhausting that it is more than probable Charles and Diana were *not* hoping for them.

In January 1984 the papers did an about-turn. Tired of the craze for baby-spotting, they now began to explain why the Princess was intending *not* to have another baby for quite some time. 'At the moment she is still not quite confident enough to commit herself to anything which would separate her from her husband, even temporarily,' reported the *News of the World*. In fact the Princess of Wales had fooled them all and shown her confidence and her commitment in her own way, by becoming pregnant just 'when everyone was least expecting it', as her brother, 19-year-old Charles, Viscount Althorp proudly put it. He added that it was well known in the family that she wanted another child quickly.

The news that 'the royal breeding programme' really was underway was received with great delight, not least by the workers at the Jaguar car plant in Coventry, where the royal couple made their first public appearance together after Buckingham Palace had made the announcement. When Prince Charles complimented bench worker Terry McCauley on the state of affairs at the car company: 'You're doing very good work here, production is going well,' he was taken aback to receive congratulations in return. 'Your production line is going well too,' said Mr McCauley. Blushing amidst the laughter, Charles attempted to cover his confusion with a goodbye line: 'Keep up the good work,' only to be told: 'You and all, mate.' And in token of Jaguar's approval of the production line at Kensington Palace, they began work on a special new product – a one-off modelled down Jaguar pedal car for Prince William's second birthday to match the one Charles had ordered for himself on his February visit.

Humour has never been lacking from the affection the British show for their Royals. No sooner had the news of Diana's pregnancy been announced, than a bookie offered odds of 1000 to 1 on the name 'Spike',

Below left: Diana and her young son go walking to meet the press in the garden of Kensington Palace – and for once it is William's dress, not his mother's, the fashion pundits have their eyes on.
Below right: A modern addition to the traditional royal calendar of duties and pleasures – the annual skiing trip Charles and Diana take. They were staying with the royal family of Liechtenstein.

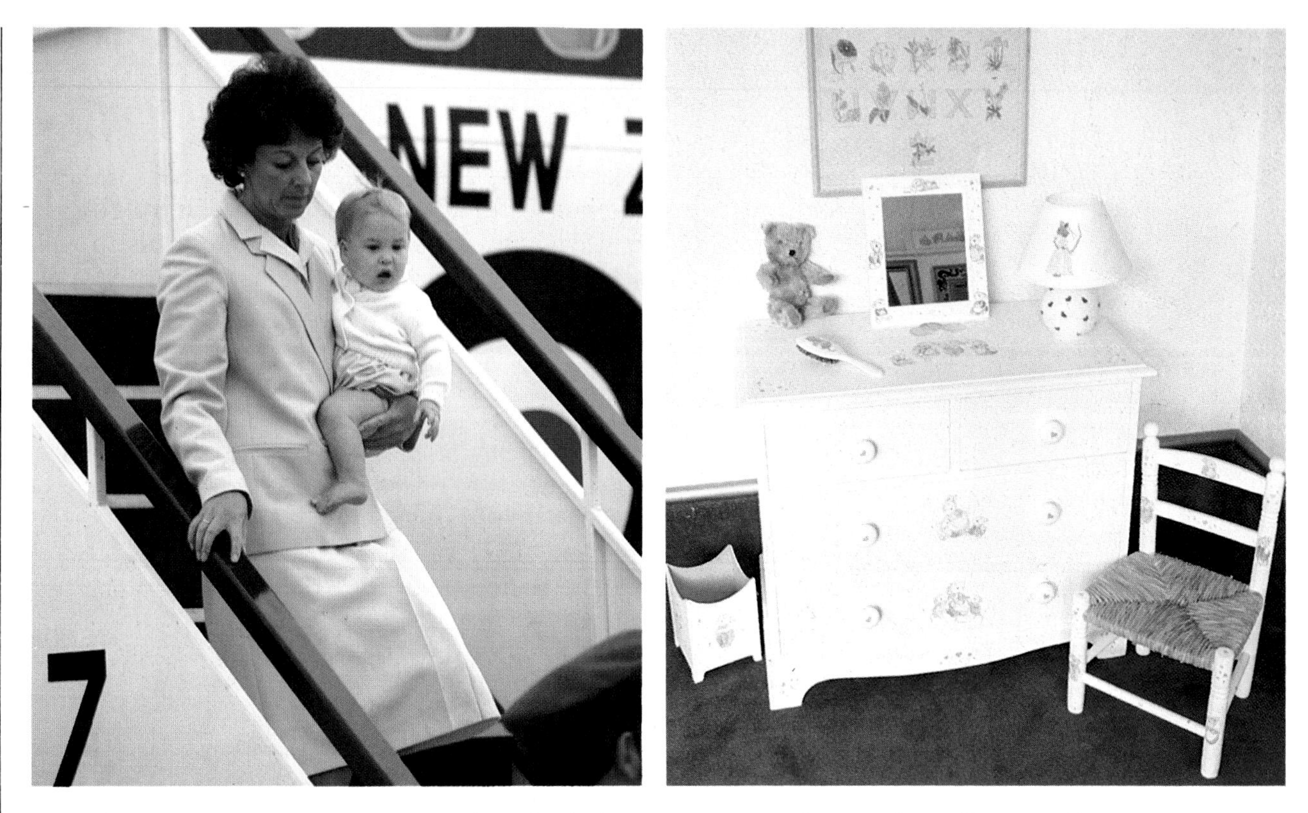

Above left: The twentieth-century prince arrives by air in Auckland, safe in the arms of nanny Barbara Barnes.
Above right: The royal baby has pretty painted furniture in his nursery at Kensington Palace.

after Charles' favourite comedian, Spike Milligan. Milligan was the man who entertained the Prince at the Lyric Theatre with jokes about his sister, her husband and Barbara Cartland, summing up the evening with an updated version of the National Anthem: 'God save our gracious Queen, Prince Philip, Charles, Di and the kid'.

Only Charles and Diana know how large they would like their family to be, but the public cannot help speculating that Diana might follow the example of her predecessor Alexandra, Princess of Wales, and have seven children without producing any more serious consequences to the populace – despite the fears of professors of demography – than a great deal of pleasure and a quantity of souvenir booklets. The desire for a large family is not the only thing that unites these two Princesses of Wales. Despite the helicopters on the lawns and the mass of security gadgets surrounding her residences, Diana's whole life is far closer to that of Alexandra's a full century ago than it is to many of her subjects. In Diana's home Alexandra would find the household rather shrunk, perhaps, but still familiar. The lady's maid, Evelyn Dagley, the one-time Buckingham Palace parlourmaid who was promoted to caring for Diana's huge wardrobes of taffeta ballgowns, silken day dresses, jaunty small veiled hats and neat kid shoes, wears jeans instead of a starched apron and grey dress, but she deals with a wardrobe not dissimilar in its contents and uses from Alexandra's own.

There are still nannies in the nursery – Barbara Barnes, also less formally dressed than she would have been a century ago, but still performing much the same role, with the help of an under nanny, Mrs Olga Powell. Diana might bath her babies herself to the sound of rock music on the radio, but the nursery staff make it possible for her to be a working mother. The recent butler, Manchester-born Mr Alan Fisher, enlivened his traditional role at the door of Diana's Kensington Palace home by greeting visitors in sneakers beneath his pin stripes, a habit he claims to have picked up while working for Bing Crosby. Alexandra would also be familiar with the concept of a country residence, Highgrove House near Tetbury, with its capacious grounds and land (348 acres), horses in the stables and fine works of art on the walls, though the swimming pool would not have been there in her day. The Wales' apartment in Kensington Palace may have a fine Georgian staircase and ample accommodation for a small family and staff, but it is still not as fine as the house in which Alexandra entertained when she was Princess of Wales in Victoria's reign. The heir to the throne and his wife, who was as famous throughout the land for her love of children as Diana is today, occupied the majestic Marlborough House near St James' Palace, a stone's throw away from Clarence House, so familiar to our Princess as the residence of her grandmother-in-law.

Even Diana's social calendar is based on the same fixed paths as Alexandra's: Ascot in June, Cowes in August, Scotland in autumn – the same Balmoral with its tartan carpets, where Diana's children will learn, as Alexandra's did, the traditional sports of hunting, shooting and

Below: Prince Charles took a keen interest in his son long before his birth, according to Diana, who claimed he was reading too many books on babies and was telling her what to do. His close involvement with his children's early years is thoroughly modern – and a great change from the days when royal fathers only saw their children for a few minutes a day, and then safely guarded by nannies. This family photograph was taken just before the Australian tour, in their Kensington Palace apartment. The wallpaper is printed with the Prince of Wales' feathers.

fishing. The January skiing trips and yearly visits to the Caribbean are modern, though equally regular additions to the Princess of Wales' calendar. These jaunts further afield would not surprise the fun-loving Alexandra as much as the batteries of cameras outside Diana's gate and the Sony headphones and rollerskates she is said to wear. Diana moves with the times, but the job description of the Princess of Wales has altered very little.

It is probably partly because her role is steeped in tradition that the Princess is seen as such an attractive figure. In a crinoline skirt and a Saudi prince's ransom in diamonds and sapphires she looks just like everbody's idea of a romantic Princess from a historical novel come to life. There is not much enthusiasm in Britain for the pedestrian sort of royalty found elsewhere on the Continent, and that is something else the Princess seems to sense instinctively. Both her job and her person symbolise tradition, and this is what her people want.

Even Prince William hardly looked like a child of his time when he was first displayed for the camera. Clad in the hand-smocked silks his mother chose for the occasion, he bore a closer resemblance to the Prince Charles of 35 years before, than to most of his contemporaries, crawling about in their brightly coloured stretch romper suits. The similarity between father and son underlined the continuity in the Royal Family: this baby was special, and no-one wanted to pretend otherwise.

The appeal of William and his mother is so special, in fact, that to be a member of the aristocracy, a stratum of society that was despised and ignored throughout the 1960s, has suddenly become highly fashionable, and the style of the so-called Sloane Ranger is now immensely popular and much copied. The Princess of Wales has been christened the Super-Sloane, but under this new name lies the age-old fascination with aristocracy that Diana has made respectable again to the middle classes. Twenty years ago it was suppressed. A hundred years ago there was no pretence about it.

This return to fashion has meant that Prince Charles, who seemed so out of place in the 60s in his brogues and tweeds and earnest attitudes, has suddenly found himself in his maturity to be a man of his times. And the return to an emphasis on the importance of traditional values is a return to his own views, solidly rooted as they are in a conservative approach to institutions, liberal ideals, and an absolute conviction of the necessity of a solid family life. Charles' family life is deeply rooted in history and William, who is by all accounts a forceful baby, has brought this home to his father more clearly than ever before. Charles described it like this: 'Suddenly you find that your child is not a malleable object or an offprint of yourself, but is the culmination of goodness knows how many thousands of years and genetic make-up of your ancestors.'

In his knowledge of his own children's thousands of years of genetic make-up the Prince is undoubtedly uniquely well placed. But in his appreciation of each child's unique preciousness he is voicing the sentiments of every parent. The way people identify with the Wales family is the reason why there is, and will continue to be, such a tremendous response to the Children's Princess and the Princess' children.

Right: Sparkling, despite a second pregnancy which she found very tiring from its earliest stages, Diana dressed for evening in an historically inspired gown with high waist, low neckline and detailed sleeves which are very flattering in maternity.

CHAPTER TWO

A Way with Children

From the first moment Lady Diana Spencer went walkabout, after the announcement of her engagement to the Prince of Wales, it was clear that children were her first love. Photographs showed Diana breaking through the formality that had up till then existed even on informal walkabouts. Spontaneous, charming, obviously happy, she was seen crouching on the ground, silk skirts trailing in the dirt, chatting to toddlers, hugging small ice-cream besmeared brats who held up their arms to her, coo-ing over babies, and swapping jokes with 10-year-olds as though the whole lot of them were a set of small cousins she hadn't seen for a few days.

To the surprise of some observers, the spectacle continued. A hundred walkabouts later the fully fledged Princess, who had learned how to stand on her dignity with the press, was kissing and cuddling the nation's children with an enthusiasm that showed she was as besotted as ever. Now the line of tiny royal fans below handshake-level is such a familiar sight that it is hardly remarked on. They all clutch posies wrapped in silver foil, and the Princess will gratefully accept them, or coax one from an unwilling hand if the giver is overcome with stage-fright. The children know that they will be the first to receive Diana's attention – and to make absolutely certain of it, they will spend hours crayoning in bright banners 'We love you, Princess Di', or the name of their school, with a message of welcome.

Even those who work with children are delighted and amazed by the natural rapport Diana has with them. A typical comment came after her visit to the Great Ormond Street Hospital for Sick Children in December 1982. 'She was absolutely marvellous with the children and the staff loved her,' said the House Governor, Mr Bill Milchen. 'She is so very natural. She has a way with children that is truly fantastic.' Mr Milchen was expressing his conversion to the huge multitude of Diana's fans. And their hearts are touched not only by her strong maternal instincts, but also by the shyness she felt when she was first on public display.

With the world's cameras on her, a posse of policemen at her heels, and thousands of strangers scrutinizing her every movement, the 19-year-old Lady Diana Spencer took refuge in talking to those with whom she felt most at ease: children. Before her marriage she had had little outward success. She had not shone at school, or in finding a job she liked enough to stick at afterwards. And despite her strong character and insatiable interest in people, there had been very little in her life to build up her confidence in her abilities. In all probability, shyness as well as kindness lay behind her request on her first visit to the school at Tetbury, to skip coffee with the teachers so that she could spend more time with the children. A hearfelt gesture, no doubt, and one that was much appreciated. But the thought of speaking to adults in awe of her position and putting them at their ease must have been more terrifying for a teenager unused to her role than chatting with children. With

Above: On the streets of Tetbury, in May 1981, the then Lady Diana Spencer showed the informality and love of children which were to be the hallmark of royal walkabouts thereafter. Above right: Knee-level talks at Broadlands at a tree planting ceremony. This habit of conversing at grassroots took security men by surprise on Diana's first public appearances with her husband-to-be.

Previous page: Flags and flowers and a row of small hands at every level – familiar sights at each Diana walkabout. This one was in Canberra during her Australian tour.

children she could be herself, because they would be completely themselves with her.

Her confidence with children was securely based. From her earliest years, when she had helped look after her baby brother Charles, she had demonstrated her talents in that direction. Before her engagement she had worked as an unpaid nanny for friends, as well as at the Young England kindergarten. At school at West Heath near Sevenoaks she used to go for one afternoon a week to a home for the handicapped to play with the children and help out the busy staff. She also used to call each week on an old lady to do her shopping and help around the house, and it was noticeable that, after children, Diana sought out the old to chat to as comfortable and familiar friends. Once she began to accept engagements on her own account, homes for old people as well as children's hospitals and homes became a priority on her official schedule. The Princess of Wales is the Chelsea Pensioners' favourite pin-up. 'Forget Vera Lynn, forget Lilian Gish,' said 84-year-old RSM John McLellan when she visited the Royal Hospital in December 1983, 'the Princess of Wales has taken over.'

The love between Diana and the people began because both sides needed and wanted each other. And a great part of the reason for Diana's success with young and old is that the affection is kept on an equal footing. The toddlers are hugged and kissed in a way which suggests that it is as much a treat for her as it is for them. Diana avoids the

Right: The Princess of Wales meets a young Welshman on her visit to Brecon after her honeymoon. Moments later he received one of those precious royal kisses that children were beginning to clamour for.

run of patronizing adult questions about names and ages, and what they will do when they're grown up. Instead she drops down from her 5' 10" to eye-level contact – her long full skirts must often be chosen with her small fans in mind – and swaps information. She teases and sympathises: 'I wasn't much good at music, I couldn't cope with sight-reading,' she told one child when she visited the Children's Youth Orchestra in April 1984. She shows she understands about the difficulties of being bossed by elder sisters. She has been known to ask for a fruit gum, even a loan. 'Can I have your 10p to get me home?' she asked an appalled three-year-old on her tour of Great Ormond Street Hospital, and grinned as Ben Walford stoutly refused to hand over his cash.

With her pregnancy and the birth of William she found another group with whom she achieved instant rapport. 'Oh the joy of things to come!' she said enviously to a mother holding her young baby in her arms in the Scilly Isles, and once the joy had duly arrived she was chatting to all the mothers she came across about the difficulties of teething problems and of bringing up children, in a way which quite brushed aside any embarrassment they might have had speaking to a Princess. She has an invaluable gift for identifying with those she meets, no doubt partly because she has not suffered from the handicap of being born a princess, distant and apart. And though she was at first shy of public functions, possible mishaps, and public speaking, she was never in the slightest bit embarrassed when children broke protocol. A laugh was

Above: Gloveless in spite of the cold, the Princess of Wales delightedly greets two small and well muffled admirers in Oslo. The news of her second pregnancy was yet to be announced.

her only response when a three-year-old tried to pull her hat off at a visit to a hospital in Wrexham.

When she called for tea at a former council flat on the Easterhouse estate in Glasgow, she was more at ease than her hostess. 'I expect I'll be vacuuming and dusting right up to the last moment,' said Mrs Helen McAllen on the eve of her call. 'The children make such a mess.' When the Princess settled down on the sofa with her cup of weak tea and a sliver of strawberry gateau the dreaded happened. Two-year-old Barry moved in. 'I'm afraid that Barry tried to eat the Princess's cake as she was having her tea,' said his mother, 'but she coped beautifully.' Diana posed for a photograph for the family album with the rest of the children afterwards.

For the children, she is the stuff of fairy tales, appearing as if by magic in their street, good, beautiful, kind, and fond of them, as princesses are supposed to be. Perhaps because like them she once dreamed about princesses herself, Diana quite understands how her young fans see her. Five-year-old Samantha Markby, who went to see the Princess in Camberley in 1982, put it like this: 'I like Princess Diana because she's beautiful and she smiles a lot. I'd like to tell her I love her. I think Princess Diana is like a fairy Princess. I'd like to blow her a kiss but I can't send it because I don't know where she is and it would get lost.'

The occasional child might be disappointed because she is not actually carrying a wand, but Diana is aware that a good number fully

Above: Despite the officialdom and pomp surrounding every visit, Diana somehow manages to make each child she talks to feel she has her full, natural, and special attention. This time she is at the Fisher Price Toy Factory at Peterlee in County Durham.

expect to see her dressed with diamonds in broad daylight. On a visit to Carlisle she apologized to eight-year-old Gerald Beedle for wearing her fetching little grey tip-tilted hat instead of a crown, 'He has dirty sticky hands,' said Gerald's teacher in warning, as the child stretched out his arms to touch her, but the warning went ignored, as usual. Diana is not shy of contact and more often than not goes without gloves. She once gave back a glove a three-year-old had dropped on the road with the comment: 'It's a vital piece of equipment in this weather.' But though it was chilly, the Princess herself was barehanded. The reason she does not follow the example of her mother-in-law – the Queen wears gloves for walkabouts even in tropical climes – may have something to do with the tradition set when she was Lady Diana Spencer and every child and its mother wanted to see the sapphire engagement ring. But it probably has more to do with her desire to cut down the barriers of formality between herself and the children who welcome her.

She will be seen straightening a child's crooked tie, or coaxing a fallen red wellington boot back onto a little foot with a cheerful 'Musn't let your tootsies get cold!', or admonishing a shy toddler: 'Don't suck your thumb, or your teeth will fall out!' Amidst all the pomp and ceremony, it is the Princess who notices when things are going wrong: it was she who spotted a boy being crushed against a crowd barrier on a visit to Newcastle in March 1982. 'I got my legs stuck against a crush bar as the crowd pushed forward. I fell down, but the next thing I knew

Overleaf: Red roses for 'I love you' – children give them to Diana wherever she goes. Here it is a small girl in the crowd at the Hearsay Centre in Catford.